The telling or reading of ghost stories during long, dark, and cold Christmas nights is a yuletide ritual dating back to at least the eighteenth century, and was once as much a part of Christmas tradition as decorating fir trees, feasting on goose, and the singing of carols. During the Victorian era many magazines printed ghost stories specifically for the Christmas season. These "winter tales" didn't necessarily explore Christmas themes. Rather, they were offered as an eerie pleasure to be enjoyed on Christmas Eve with the family, adding a supernatural shiver to the seasonal chill.

The tradition remained strong in the British Isles (and her colonies) throughout much of the twentieth century, though in recent years it has been on the wane. Certainly, few people in Canada or the United States seem to know about it any longer. This series of small books seeks to rectify this, to revive a charming custom for the long, dark nights we all know so well here at Christmastime.

Charles Dickens
The Signalman

A.M. Burrage
One Who Saw

Edith Wharton
Afterward

M.R. James
The Diary of Mr. Poynter

Marjorie Bowen
The Crown Derby Plate

E.F. Benson
How Fear Departed the Long Gallery

W.W. Jacobs
The Toll House

Algernon Blackwood
The Empty House

H. Russell Wakefield
The Red Lodge

Frank Cowper
Christmas Eve on a Haunted Hulk

R.H. Malden
The Sundial

Elizabeth Gaskell
The Old Nurse's Story

Daphne du Maurier
The Apple Tree

Richard Bridgeman
The Morgan Trust

M.R. James
The Story of a Disappearance and an Appearance

Walter de la Mare
The Green Room

Margaret Oliphant
The Open Door

Bernard Capes
An Eddy on the Floor

F. Marion Crawford
The Doll's Ghost

Edith Wharton
Mr. Jones

Shirley Jackson
A Visit

Cynthia Asquith
The Corner Shop

Gertrude Atherton
The Dead and the Countess

Arthur Conan Doyle
The Captain of the Polestar

Marjorie Bowen
The House by the Poppy Field

Andrew Caldecott
A Room in a Rectory

L.P. Hartley
Podolo

Laurence Whistler
Captain Dalgety Returns

Mary Fitt
The Amethyst Cross

PODOLO

PODOLO

L. P. HARTLEY

A GHOST STORY FOR CHRISTMAS

DESIGNED & DECORATED BY SETH

BIBLIOASIS

HE EVENING BEFORE we made the expedition to Podolo we talked it over, and I agreed there was nothing against it really.

"But why did you say you'd feel safer if Walter was going too?" Angela asked me. And Walter said, "What good should I be? I can't help to row the gondola, you know."

Then I felt rather silly, for everything I had said about Podolo was merely conversational exaggeration, meant to whet their curiosity, like a newspaper headline: and I knew that when Angela actually saw the dull little island, its stony and inhospitable shore littered with broken bottles and empty tins, she would think what a fool I was, with my romancing. So I took back everything I said, called my own bluff, as it were, and explained that I avoided Podolo only because of its exposed position: it was four miles from Venice, and if a boisterous bora got up (as it sometimes did, without warning) we should find getting back hard work, and might be late home. "And what will Walter say," I wound up, "if he comes back from Trieste" (he was going there for the day on business) "and finds no wife to welcome him?" Walter said, on the contrary, he had often wished such a thing might happen. And so, after some playful recriminations between this lately married, charming, devoted couple, we agreed that Podolo should be the goal for tomorrow's picnic. "You must curb my wife's generous impulses," Walter warned me; "She always wants to do something for somebody. It's an expensive habit." I assured him that at Podolo she would find no calls on her heart or her purse. Except perhaps for a rat or two, it was quite uninhabited. Next morning in brilliant sunshine Walter gulped down his breakfast and started for the station. It seemed hard that he should have to spend six hours of this divine day in a stuffy train. I stood on the balcony watching his departure.

The sunlight sparkled on the water; the gondola, in its best array, glowed and glittered. "Say good-bye to Angela for me," cried Walter as the gondolier braced himself for the first stroke. "And what is your postal address at Podolo?" "Full fathom five," I called out, but I don't think my reply reached him.

* * *

UNTIL YOU GET right up to Podolo you can form no estimate of its size. There is nothing nearby to compare it with. On the horizon it looks like a foot rule. Even now, though I have been there many times, I cannot say whether it is a hundred yards long or two hundred. But I have no wish to go back and make certain.

We cast anchor a few feet from the stony shore. Podolo, I must say, was looking its best, green, flowery, almost welcoming. One side is rounded to form the shallow arc of a circle: the other is straight. Seen from above, it must look like the moon in its first quarter. Seen as we saw it from the waterline with the grassy rampart behind, it forms a kind of natural amphitheatre. The slim withy-like acacia trees give a certain charm to the foreground, and to the back-ground, where they grow in clumps, and cast darker shadows, an air of mystery. As we sat in the gondola we were like theatre-goers in the stalls, staring at an empty stage.

It was nearly two o'clock when we began lunch. I was very hungry, and, charmed by my companion and occupied by my food, I did not let my eyes stray out of the boat. To Angela belonged the honour of discovering the first denizen of Podolo.

"Why," she exclaimed, "there's a cat." Sure enough there was: a little cat, hardly more than a kitten, very thin and scraggy, and mewing with automatic regularity every two or three seconds. Standing on the weedy stones at the water's edge, it was a pitiful sight. "It's smelt the food," said Angela. "It's hungry. Probably it's starving."

Mario, the gondolier, had also made the discovery, but he received it in a different spirit. "*Povera bestia*," he cried in sympathetic accents, but his eyes brightened. "Its owners did not want it. It has been put here on purpose, one sees." The idea that the cat had been left to starve caused him no great concern, but it shocked Angela profoundly.

"How abominable!" she exclaimed. "We must take it something to eat at once."

The suggestion did not recommend itself to Mario, who had to haul up the anchor and see the prospect of his own lunch growing more remote: I too thought we might wait till the meal was over. The cat would not die before our eyes. But Angela could brook no delay. So, to the accompaniment of a good deal of stamping and heavy breathing, the prow of the gondola was turned to land.

Meanwhile the cat continued to meow, though it had retreated a little and was almost invisible, a thin wisp of tabby fur, against the parched stems of the outermost grasses.

Angela filled her hand with chicken bones.

"I shall try to win its confidence with these," she said, "and then if I can I shall catch it and put it in the boat and we'll take it to Venice. If it's left here, it'll certainly starve."

She climbed along the knife-like gunwale of the gondola and stepped delicately on to the slippery boulders.

Continuing to eat my chicken in comfort, I watched her approach the cat. It ran away, but only a few yards: its hunger was obviously keeping its fear at bay. She threw a bit of food and it came nearer: another, and it came nearer still. Its demeanour grew less suspicious; its tail rose into the air; it came right up to Angela's feet. She pounced. But the cat was too quick for her; it slipped through her hands like water. Again hunger overpowered mistrust. Back it came. Once more Angela made a grab at it; once more it eluded her. But the third time, she was successful. She got hold of its leg.

I shall never forget seeing it dangle from Angela's (fortunately) gloved hand. It wriggled and squirmed and fought, and in spite of its tiny size the violence of its struggles made Angela quiver like a twig in a gale. And all the while it made the most extraordinary noise, the angriest, wickedest sound I ever heard. Instead of growing louder as its fury mounted, the sound actually decreased in volume, as though the creature was being choked by its own rage. The spitting died away into the thin ghost of a snarl, infinitely malevolent, but hardly more audible from where I was than the hiss of air from a punctured tire.

Mario was distressed by what he felt to be Angela's brutality. "Poor beast!" he exclaimed with pitying looks. "She ought not to treat it like that." And his face gleamed with satisfaction when, intimidated by the whirling claws, she let the cat drop. It streaked away into the grass, its belly to the ground.

Angela climbed back into the boat. "I nearly had it," she said, her voice still unsteady from the encounter. "I think I shall get it next time. Or shall throw a coat over it." She ate her asparagus in silence, throwing the stalks over the side. I saw that she was preoccupied and couldn't get the cat out of her mind. Any form of suffering in others affected her almost like an illness. I began to wish we hadn't come to Podolo; it was not the first time a picnic there had gone badly.

"I tell you what," Angela said suddenly. "If I can't catch it, I'll kill it. It's only a question of dropping one of these boulders on it. I could do it quite easily." She disclosed her plan to Mario, who was horror-struck. His code was different from hers. He did not mind the animal dying of slow starvation; that was in the course of nature. But deliberately to kill it! "*Poveretto!* It has done no one any harm," he exclaimed with indignation. But there was another reason, I suspected, for his attitude. Venice is overrun with cats, chiefly because it is considered unlucky to kill them. If they fall into the water and are drowned, so much the better, but woe betide whoever pushes them in.

I expounded the gondolier's point of view to Angela, but she was not impressed. "Of course I don't expect him to do it," she said, "nor you either, if you'd rather not. It may be a messy business, but it will soon be over. Poor little brute, it's in a horrible state. Its life can't be any pleasure to it."

"But we don't know that," I urged, still cravenly averse from the deed of blood. "If it could speak, it might say it preferred to live at all costs." But I couldn't move Angela from her purpose.

"Let's go and explore the island," she said, "until it's time to bathe. The cat will have got over its fright and be hungry again by then, and I'm sure I shall be able to catch it. I promise I won't murder it except as a last resource."

The word "murder" lingered unpleasantly in my mind as we made our survey of the island. You couldn't imagine a better place for one. During the war a battery had been mounted there. The concrete emplacement, about as long as a tennis court, remained: but nature and the weather had conspired to break it up, leaving black holes large enough to admit a man. These holes were like crevasses in a glacier, but masked by vegetation instead of snow. Even in the brilliant afternoon sunlight one had to tread cautiously. "Perhaps the cat has its

lair down there," I said, indicating a gloomy cavern with a jagged edge. "I suppose its eye would shine in the dark." Angela lay down on the pavement and peered in. "I thought I heard something move," she said, "but it might be anywhere in this rabbit warren."

Our bathe was a great success. The water was so warm one hardly felt the shock of going in. The only drawback was the mud, which clung to Angela's white bathing shoes, nasty sticky stuff. A little wind had got up. But the grassy rampart sheltered us; we leaned against it and smoked. Suddenly I noticed it was past five.

"We ought to go soon," I said. "We promised, do you remember, to send the gondola to meet Walter's train."

"All right," said Angela, "just let me have a go at the cat first. Let's put the food" (we had brought some remnants of lunch with us) "here where we last saw it, and watch."

There was no need to watch, for the cat appeared at once and made for the food. Angela and I stole up behind it, but I inadvertently kicked a stone and the cat was off like a flash. Angela looked at me reproachfully. "Perhaps you could manage better alone," I said. Angela seemed to think she could. I retreated a few yards, but the cat, no doubt scenting a trap, refused to come out.

Angela threw herself on the pavement. "I can see it," she muttered. "I must win its confidence again. Give me three minutes and I'll catch it."

Three minutes passed. I felt concerned for Angela, her lovely hair floating over the dark hole, her face, as much as one could see of it, a little red. The air was getting chilly.

"Look here," I said, "I'll wait for you in the gondola. When you've caught it, give a shout and I'll have the boat brought to land." Angela nodded; she dare not speak for fear of scaring her prey.

So I returned to the gondola. I could just see the line of Angela's shoulders; her face, of course, was hidden. Mario stood up, eagerly watching the chase. "She loves it so much," he said, "that she wants to kill it." I remembered Oscar Wilde's epigram, rather uncomfortably; still, nothing could be more disinterested than Angela's attitude to the cat. "We ought to start," the gondolier warned me. "The signore will be waiting at the station and wonder what has happened."

"What about Walter?" I called across the water. "He won't know what to do."

Her mind was clearly on something else as she said: "Oh, he'll find his own way home."

More minutes passed. The gondolier smiled. "One must have patience with ladies," he said; "always patience."

I tried a last appeal. "If we started at once we could just do it." She didn't answer. Presently I called out again. "What luck, Angela? Any hope of catching him?"

There was a pause: then I heard her say, in a curiously tense voice. "I'm not trying to *catch* him now."

The need for immediate hurry had passed, since we were irrevocably late for Walter. A sense of relaxation stole over me; I wrapped the rug round me to keep off the treacherous cold sirocco and I fell asleep. Almost at once, it seemed, I began to dream. In my dream it was night; we were hurrying across the lagoon trying to be in time for Walter's train. It was so dark I could see nothing but the dim blur of Venice ahead, and the little splash of whitish water where the oar dipped. Suddenly I stopped rowing and looked round. The seat behind me seemed to be empty. "Angela!" I cried;

but there was no answer. I grew frightened. "Mario!" I shouted. "Where's the signora? We have left her behind! We must go back at once!" The gondolier, too, stopped rowing and came towards me; I could just distinguish his face; it had a wild look. "She's there, signore," he said. "But where? She's not on the seat." "She wouldn't stay on it," said the gondolier. And then, as is the way in dreams, I knew what his next words would be. "We loved her and so we had to kill her."

An uprush of panic woke me. The feeling of relief at getting back to actuality was piercingly sweet. I was restored to the sunshine. At least I thought so, in the ecstasy of returning consciousness. The next moment I began to doubt, and an uneasiness, not unlike the beginning of a nightmare, stirred in me again. I opened my eyes to the daylight, but they didn't receive it. I looked out onto darkness. At first I couldn't believe my eyes:

I wondered if I was fainting. But a glance at my watch explained everything. It was past seven o'clock. I had slept the brief twilight through and now it was night, though a few gleams lingered in the sky over Fusina.

Mario was not to be seen. I stood up and looked round. There he was on the poop, his knees drawn up, asleep. Before I had time to speak he opened his eyes, like a dog.

"Signore," he said, "you went to sleep, so I did too." To sleep out of hours is considered a joke all the world over; we both laughed. "But the signora," he said. "Is *she* asleep? Or is she still trying to catch the cat?"

We strained our eyes towards the island, which was much darker than the surrounding sky.

"That's where she was," said Mario, pointing, "but I can't see her now."

"Angela!" I called.

There was no answer, indeed no sound at all but the noise of the waves slapping against the gondola.

We stared at each other.

"Let us hope she has taken no harm," said Mario, a note of anxiety in his voice. "The cat was very fierce, but it wasn't big enough to hurt her, was it?"

"No, no," I said. "It might have scratched her when she was putting her face—you know—into one of those holes."

"She was trying to kill it, wasn't she?" asked Mario. I nodded.

"*Ha fatto male*," said Mario. "In this country we are not accustomed to kill cats."

"*You* call, Mario," I said impatiently. "Your voice is stronger than mine."

Mario obeyed with a shout that might have raised the dead.

But no answer came.

"Well," I said briskly, trying to conceal

my agitation, "we must go and look for her or else we shall be late for dinner, and the signore will be getting worried. She must be a—a heavy sleeper."

Mario didn't answer.

"*Avanti!*" I said. "*Andiamo! Coraggio!*" I could not understand why Mario, usually so quick to execute an order, did not move. He was staring straight in front of him.

"There is someone on the island," he said at last, "but it's not the signora."

I must say, to do us justice, that within a couple of minutes we had beached the boat and landed. To my surprise Mario kept the oar in his hand. "I have a pocket-knife," he remarked, "but the blade is only so long," indicating the third joint of a stalwart little finger.

"It was a man, then?" said I.

"It looked like a man's head."

"But you're not sure?"

"No, because it didn't walk like a man."

"How then?"

Mario bent forward and touched the ground with his free hand. I couldn't imagine why a man should go on all fours, unless he didn't want to be seen.

"He must have come while we were asleep," I said. "There'll be a boat round the other side. But let's look here first."

We were standing by the place where we had last seen Angela. The grass was broken and bent; she had left a handkerchief as though to mark the spot. Otherwise there was no trace of her.

"Now let's find his boat," I said.

We climbed the grassy rampart and began to walk round the shallow curve, stumbling over concealed brambles.

"Not here, not here," muttered Mario.

From our little eminence we could see clusters of lights twinkling across the lagoon;

Fusina three or four miles away on the left, Malamocco the same distance on the right. And straight ahead, Venice, floating on the water like a swarm of fireflies. But no boat. We stared at each other, bewildered.

"So he didn't come by water," said Mario at last. "He must have been here all the time."

"But are you quite certain it wasn't the signora you saw?" I asked. "How could you tell in the darkness?"

"Because the signora was wearing a white dress," said Mario. "And this one is all in black—unless he is a Negro."

"That's why it's so difficult to see him."

"Yes, we can't see him, but he can see us, all right."

I felt a curious sensation in my spine.

"Mario," I said, "he must have seen her, you know. Do you think he's got anything to do with her not being here?"

Mario didn't answer.

"I don't understand why he doesn't speak to us."

"Perhaps he can't speak."

"But you thought he was a man … Anyhow, we are two against one. Come on. You take the right. I'll go to the left."

We soon lost sight of each other in the darkness, but once or twice I heard Mario swearing as he scratched himself on the thorny acacias. My search was more successful than I expected. Right at the corner of the island, close to the water's edge, I found one of Angela's bathing shoes: she must have taken it off in a hurry for the button was torn away. A little later I made a rather grisly discovery. It was the cat, dead, with its head crushed. The pathetic little heap of fur would never suffer the pangs of hunger again. Angela had been as good as her word.

I was just going to call Mario when

the bushes parted and something hurled itself upon me. I was swept off my feet. Alternately dragging and carrying me, my captor continued his headlong course. The next thing I knew I was pitched pell-mell into the gondola and felt the boat move under me.

"Mario!" I gasped. And then—absurd question—"What have you done with the oar?"

The gondolier's white face stared down at me.

"The oar? I left it—it wasn't any use, signore. I tried . . . What it wants is a machine gun."

He was rowing frantically with my oar: the island began to recede.

"But we can't go away!" I cried.

The gondolier said nothing, but rowed with all his strength. Then he began to talk under his breath. "It was a good oar, too,"

I heard him mutter. Suddenly he left the poop, climbed over the cushions, and sat down beside me.

"When I found her," he whispered, "she wasn't quite dead."

I began to speak but he held up his hand.

"She asked me to kill her."

"But, Mario!"

"'Before it comes back,' she said. And then she said, '*It's* starving, too, and it won't wait…'" Mario bent his head nearer but his voice was almost inaudible.

"Speak up," I cried. The next moment I implored him to stop.

Mario clambered onto the poop.

"You don't want to go to the island now, signore?"

"No, no. Straight home."

I looked back. Transparent darkness covered the lagoon save for one shadow that stained the horizon black. Podolo…

P. HARTLEY (1895–1972) was a British novelist and short story writer.

SETH'S COMICS AND drawings have appeared in the *New York Times*, the *New Yorker*, the *Globe and Mail*, and countless other publications.

His graphic novel *Clyde Fans* won the prestigious Festival d'Angoulême's Prix Spécial du Jury.

He lives in Guelph, Ontario, with his wife, Tania, in an old house he has named "Inkwell's End."

Copyright © The Trustees of the Estate
of Annie Norah Hartley, 2024

Illustrations and design copyright © Seth, 2024

All rights reserved. No part of this publication may be reproduced or transmitted in any form or by any means, electronic or mechanical, including photocopying, recording, or any information storage and retrieval system, without permission in writing from the publisher or a license from The Canadian Copyright Licensing Agency (Access Copyright). For an Access Copyright license visit www.accesscopyright.ca or call toll free to 1-800-893-5777.

Library and Archives Canada Cataloguing in Publication

Title: Podolo : a ghost story for Christmas / L.P. Hartley ; designed and decorated by Seth.
Names: Hartley, L. P. (Leslie Poles), 1895-1972, author. | Seth, 1962- illustrator.
Description: Series statement: Seth's Christmas ghost stories
Identifiers: Canadiana 20240382455 | ISBN 9781771966382 (softcover)
Subjects: LCGFT: Short stories. | LCGFT: Ghost stories.
Classification: LCC PR6015.A6723 P63 2024 | DDC 823/.912—dc23

Readied for the press by Daniel Wells
Illustrated and designed by Seth
Copyedited by Ashley Van Elswyk
Typeset by Vanessa Stauffer

PRINTED AND BOUND IN CANADA